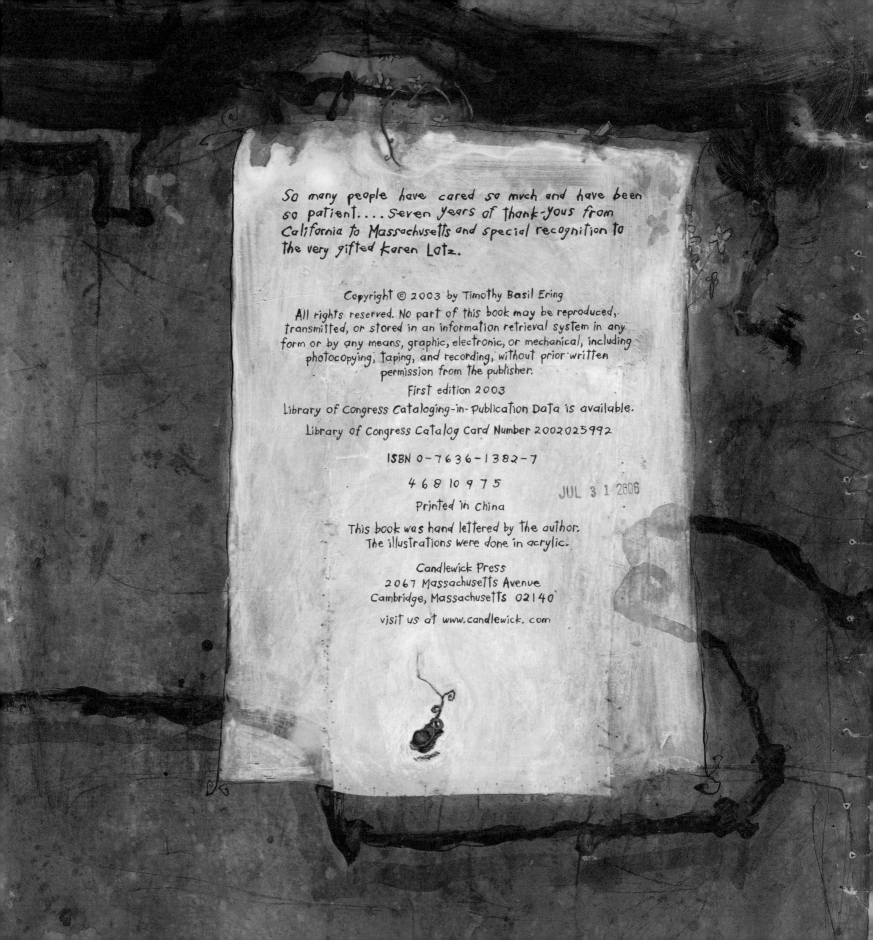

So many people have cared so much and have been so patient.... Seven years of thank-yous from California to Massachusetts and special recognition to the very gifted Karen Lotz.

First edition 2003

Library of Congress Cataloging-in-Publication Data is available.

Library of Congress Catalog Card Number 2002025992

ISBN 0-7636-1382-7

4 6 8 10 9 7 5

JUL 3 1 2006

Printed in China

This book was hand lettered by the author. The illustrations were done in acrylic.

Candlewick Press
2067 Massachusetts Avenue
Cambridge, Massachusetts 02140

visit us at www.candlewick.com

The Story of
Frog Belly Rat Bone

Timothy Basil Ering

CANDLEWICK PRESS
CAMBRIDGE, MASSACHUSETTS

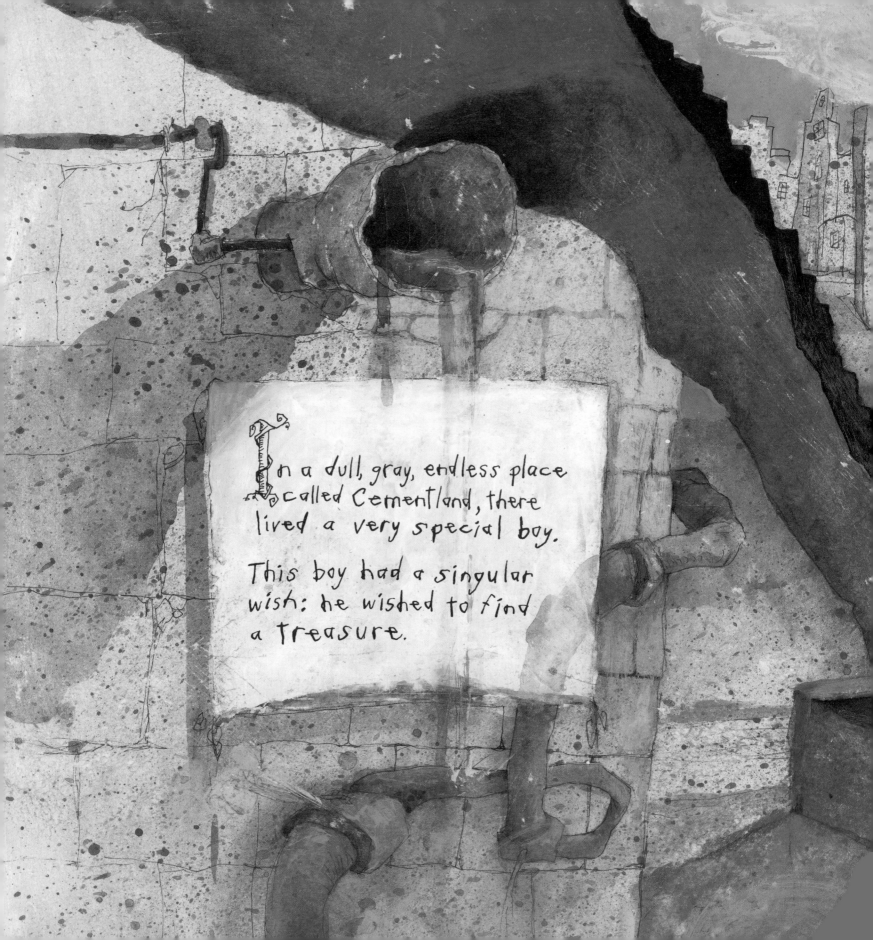

In a dull, gray, endless place called Cementland, there lived a very special boy.

This boy had a singular wish: he wished to find a treasure.

Each day the boy searched through the heaping piles of junk that collected around Cementland. He found greasy toaster ovens, broken TVs, and wet smelly socks. But no treasure.

"The only thing in these junk piles is junk!" cried the boy.

He was angry enough to give up, when all of a sudden he spied something unexpected.

It was a strange and wonderful box. Attached to the box was a wrinkled note, which said, "Put my wondrous riches into the earth and enjoy."

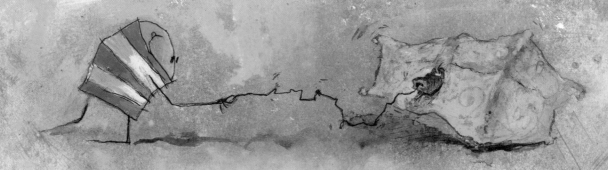

The boy pried open the lock with a twisty piece of wire and lifted the lid.

The box was bursting with dazzling colors.
"I found a treasure!" shouted the boy.

He took one of the beautiful packages
and tore it open.

But inside the package there were no bright colors at all — just hundreds of tiny gray specks. Where were all the wondrous riches?

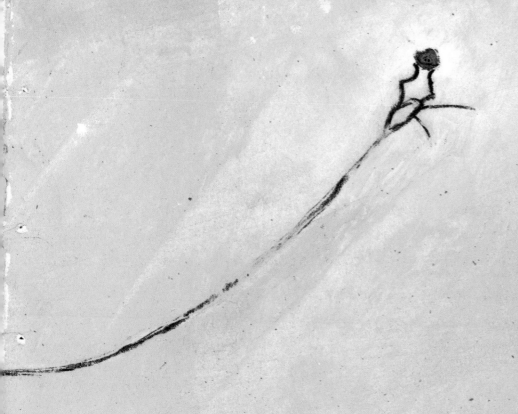

The boy wasn't sure, but he carefully prepared some earth.
He sprinkled in a few specks and waited two or three minutes.
Nothing happened.

Deeply dejected, the boy went home. He did not realize that the unguarded treasures were now in terrible danger....

The next day, the boy returned to a horrifying sight. The specks had been dug up!

"Thieves!" he screeched. In a flash, he had a plan.

He ran straight to the nearest junk pile.

There he gathered those wet smelly socks.

He found moldy pillow stuffing and scraggly wires.

He patched, buttoned, sewed, and zipped.

Soon a creature began to take shape. It had crooked bony arms and a giant-size belly.

"You'll be finished in just a second," the boy told his creation. "All you need now is a crown."

"Stand tall, Frog Belly Rat Bone!"
shouted the boy, waving his hands like a wizard.
"I dub thee king of the Treasures.
Frog Belly Rat Bone, one, two, three...
You are the monster who will protect the specks."

"Monster!" said Frog Belly Rat Bone. "But my dear boy, you've made me far too good-looking to be a monster! And by the way," he continued, "my socks are very moist, and my underwear is rather picky."

"Sorry about your underwear," said the boy. "But I need a monster to scare the thieves away from the specks— I mean the treasures."

Frog Belly wanted to see the treasures. The boy handed him a package and let him read the note.

Frog Belly sprang into the air. "My dear boy— you have found some wondrous riches! We must put them in the earth—just as the note says."

"But I already did that," said the boy. "Nothing happened."
"We'll do it again," said Frog Belly.

"Frog Belly Rat Bone,
  one, two, three...
  you must be patient
  and then you will see!"

And so Frog Belly and the boy started digging holes.
They also filled jars and cans and boxes with earth,
and sprinkled specks into each one.

They sprinkled specks all around Cementland.

When the sun began to set, it was time for the boy to go home.

"Watch out for thieves," he warned. He shook Frog Belly's hand and scurried off.

Frog Belly stood all alone in the spooky shadows. The sky grew darker and darker. Those thieves will surely be back tonight, he thought.

Just then he heard footsteps.

Someone was trying to move very carefully, stepping quietly on crinkled cans and squishy newspapers.

Frog Belly waited, not making a sound.

At that very moment, sneaking through the junk piles were three thieves — a rat, a rabbit, and a fruit fly! They were licking their chops and adjusting their masks, when an eerie voice floated toward them through the darkness.

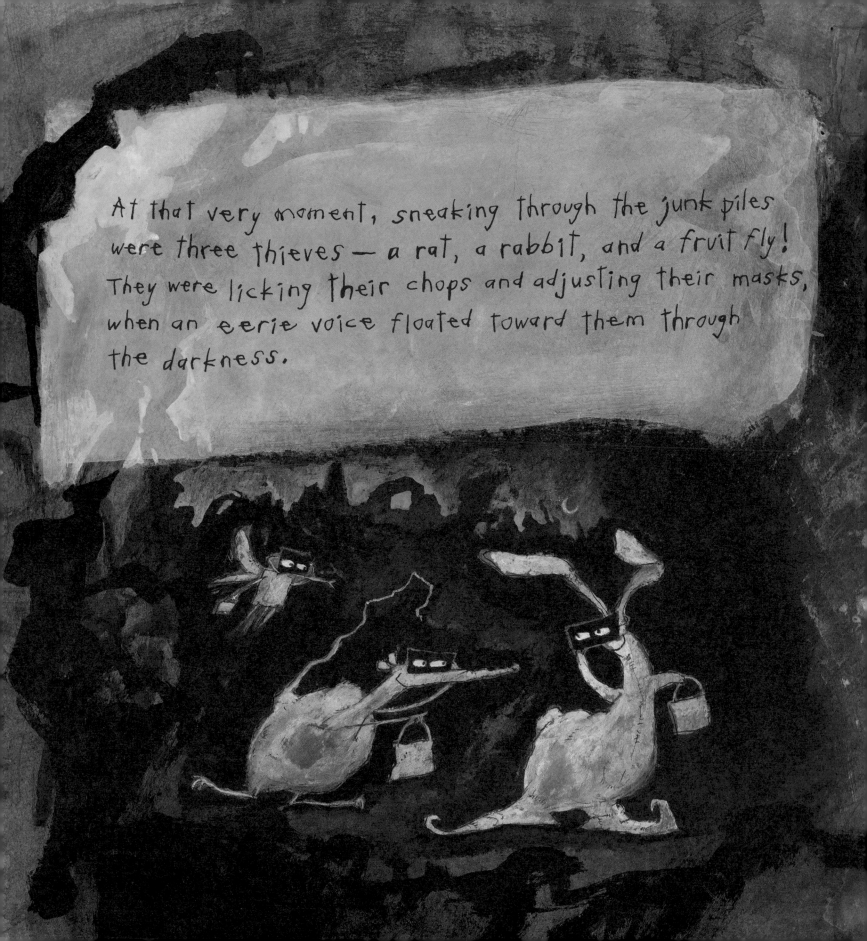

"Frog Belly Rat Bone,
one, two, three...
the specks in the earth are
protected by me.
You must be patient and then
you will see..."

"See what?" the thieves asked each other.
They were shaking in their tracks.
Just then they did see...

a giant scary monster with long bony arms and wet smelly socks!

AAAAHHH!!!

The thieves ran for their lives.

The next morning, the boy was happy to discover that Frog Belly had saved the treasures. "What do we do now?" he asked.

"Now," said Frog Belly, "We must give the treasures lots of water."

So the boy filled a watering can and went to work.

A few days later, the boy noticed something quite peculiar. The boxes were twittering. The jars and cans trembled.

"Look, Frog Belly!" he said.

Slowly and very shyly, the treasure was beginning to reveal itself.

"The wondrous riches are here at last!" Frog Belly exclaimed. Frog Belly and the boy cheered.

From inside a junk pile, the thieves were listening. They felt terrible about having tried to steal such wonderful treasures. The rabbit jumped out of the hiding place and landed right in Frog Belly's arms.

"We'll never steal again!" the rabbit cried.

"And we'll return all the specks we took!" said the fruit fly.

"Please let us help you take care of the treasures!" said the rat.

So Frog Belly and the boy forgave the thieves, and now they were all part of the team.

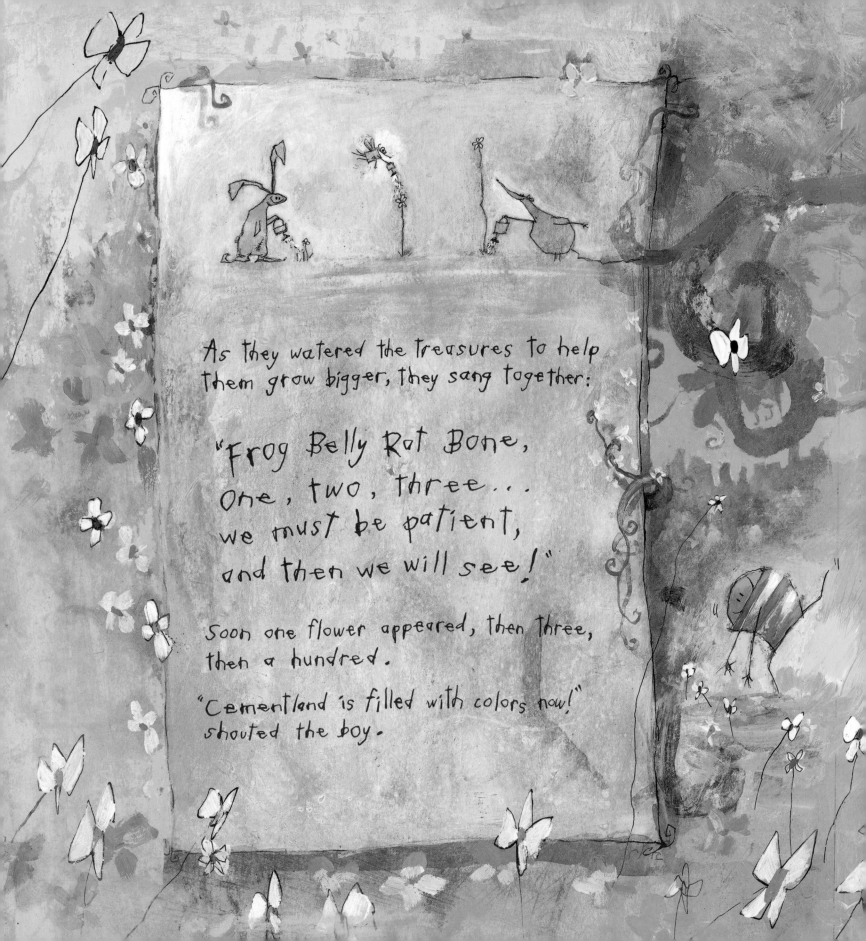

As they watered the treasures to help them grow bigger, they sang together:

"Frog Belly Rat Bone,
one, two, three...
we must be patient,
and then we will see!"

Soon one flower appeared, then three, then a hundred.

"Cementland is filled with colors now!" shouted the boy.

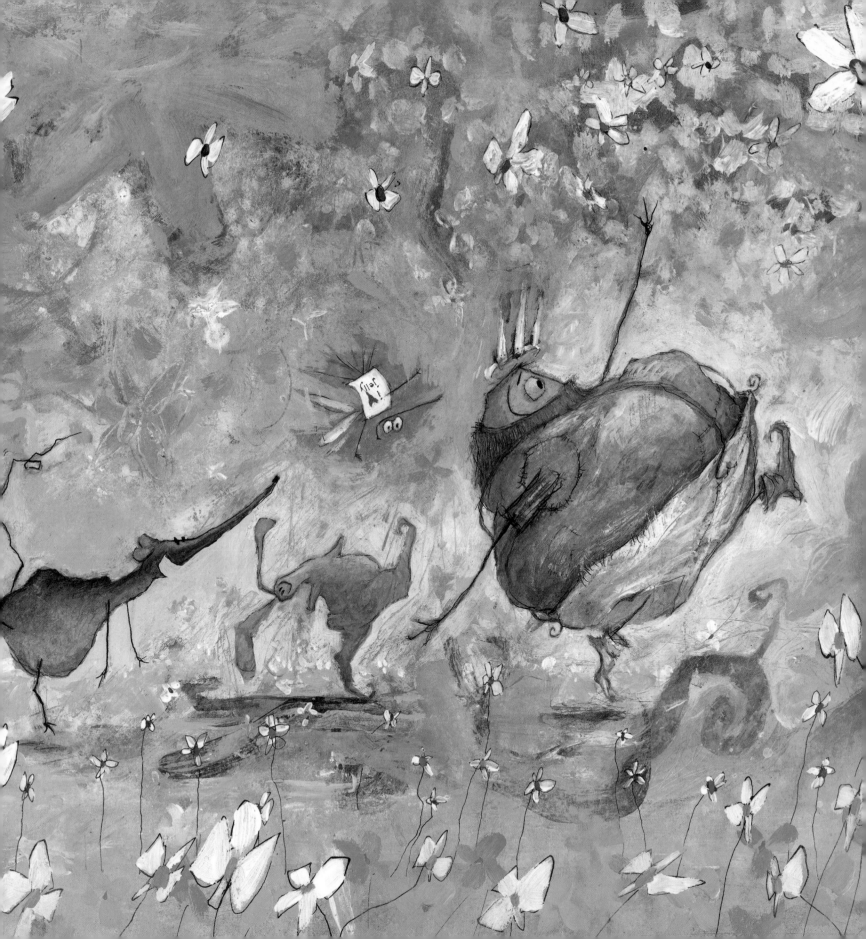

Just when it seemed that nothing better could happen, the fruit fly discovered a bright red strawberry.

"And here's a zucchini!" cried the rat.

"Go ahead, Rabbit," urged Frog Belly. "Pick the biggest carrot top you can find and pull. Pull with all your might!"

That night, the five friends prepared a special feast. A feast fit for a king!

"Three cheers for Frog Belly Rat Bone, one, two, three!"

Because thanks to Frog Belly, they were patient, and they did see.